BOOK 5

Losing Jo
by H. L. Dube

Illustrated by The Comic Stripper

Published by Ransom Publishing Ltd.
Radley House, 8 St. Cross Road, Winchester, Hampshire
SO23 9HX

www.ransom.co.uk

ISBN   978 184167 429 2
First published in 2013

STEVE SHARP

Losing Jo

by

H. L. Dube

Ransom

Steve Sharp

Steve was a cop. Now he works for himself. He is a hard man.

Jaydeen

Jaydeen works for Steve. She is in love with Steve, but never tells him.

Mrs Clayton

Mrs Clayton is rich. Her kid, Jo Clayton, is missing from home.

Jo Clayton

Jo left home to shack up with Big John, a drug dealer.

Big John

Big John makes big bucks selling drugs. He is a bad guy.

ONE

Jo Clayton and Big John are in that house.

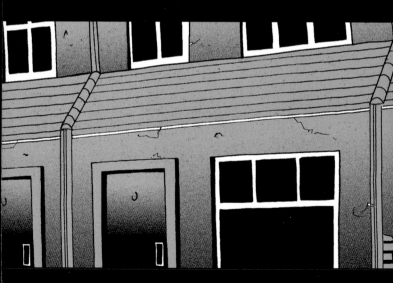

I have two jobs.

I must take Jo back to her mother.

And I must get Big John.

Jo is a kid. I have to take her away from the drug dealer.

Big John is a bad guy.

TWO

Now the shadows are getting long.
Soon it will be night.

I go to the house and look for an open window.

The front door is open. I step inside.

And all goes black.

It was Big John. He smacked me
again.

Now I am in big trouble.

'Not the shorts,' Jo says. 'Let him keep the shorts.'

I am in the back of a car. Hands
tied. Legs tied. A gag in my mouth.

I fall asleep.

THREE

I wake up when the car stops.

'Get out!' Big John says, as he pulls me out of the car.

I fall on wet grass.

A hard wind blows.

'Get in the motor, Jo!' Big John says.

'He will die up here in the cold,' Jo says.

'That is the idea,' John says, and he laughs.

He kicks my body. It is a hard kick.

John gets in the car and drives
away.

The wind is strong and hard. I feel
cold.

My hands and feet are still tied. I
must get free.

Getting free is not easy. It takes a
lot of time.

I get my hands free and then work on my feet.

I stand up. The hard wind is strong on my skin.

The grass cuts my feet.

The moon comes out in the sky. Now I can see.

I am on a windy hill, with only a pair of shorts to cover me.

No trees. No farms or houses. No roads.

I follow the tyre tracks made by Big John's car.

After a long time I come to a road.

'I must keep moving,' I say aloud.
'Keep moving, or die of cold.'

I hear the sound of a van. I wave
my arms.

The van does not stop.

FOUR

A long time passes. I am growing weak and cold. The hard road cuts my feet. I am going to die of cold. I must get help.

I see lights. The lights of a motor car. I must make the driver stop.

I stand in the road and wave my arms.

It is a police car.

The car stops and two cops get out.

One cop carries his stick.

He smacks me hard on my body with the stick.

I fall down on the hard road ...

STEVE SHARP

Now read
the next
Steve Sharp
book ....

1

2

3

4

5

6

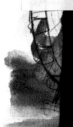

Vampire School
Ghoul Trip

For Theo and Tara
P.B.

For my friends
C.H.

First published in Great Britain in 2010 by Boxer Books Limited.
www.boxerbooks.com

Based on an original idea by Chris Harrison
Text copyright © 2010 Peter Bently
Illustrations copyright © 2010 Chris Harrison

The rights of Peter Bently to be identified as the author and
Chris Harrison as the illustrator of this work have been asserted by them
in accordance with the Copyright, Designs and Patents Act, 1988.

The illustrations were prepared using biro and watercolour paints.
The text is set in Blackmoor Plain and Adobe Caslon.

ISBN 978-1-907152-21-4

1 3 5 7 9 10 8 6 4 2

Printed in Great Britain

All of our papers are sourced from managed forests and renewable resources.

Vampire School
Ghoul Trip

Written by Peter Bently
Illustrated by Chris Harrison

Boxer Books

Contents

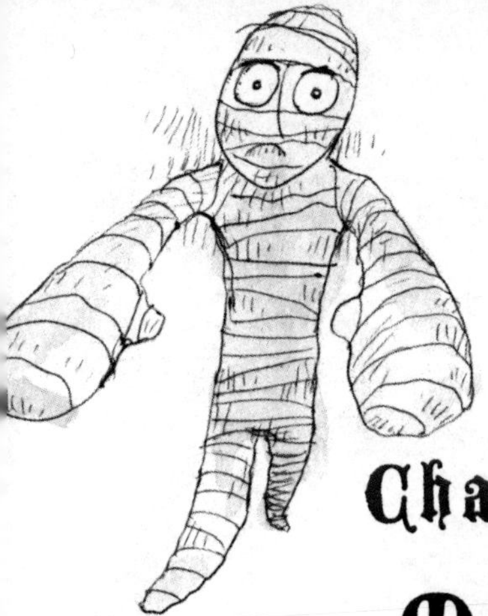

Chapter 1
A Night at the Fair

BEEP! BEEP!

Miss Gargoyle looked around at her class of young vampires. "OK everyone!" she said. "The school bus is here. Let's all make our way out in an orderly line!"

Lee Price stuck his hand up.

"Miss Gargoyle," he asked
eagerly. "Why do we have to
take the bus to the fair? Why
don't we just *fly*?"

With a sudden *POP!* Lee
turned into a bat and fluttered
around the room.

"Yes, Miss, flying would be much quicker than the bus," chipped in Bella Williams.

"*And* better for the environment," added Billy Pratt. "Bats don't make smelly fumes."

"Except when they've had beans for dinner," quipped Lee.

The class fell about laughing. Even Miss Gargoyle couldn't help grinning. She was looking forward to tonight's school trip to the funfair just as much as the children. When she was a little girl, her dad had worked on the ghost train. She used to get in for free – until he got fired for being too scary.

"We're taking the bus because it's dark and I don't want anyone to get lost on the way," she said. "Besides, I don't think it's a very good idea if twenty-five bats land in the middle of the fairground and suddenly turn into a

bunch of little vampires, do
you? You know what Fangless
folk are like. Now come along,
the bus is waiting."

Lee turned back into his normal shape and followed the rest of the class out to the school bus. On the side of the bus it said:

St. Orlok's Primary School

It used to say **for Vampires** as well, but the head teacher, Mrs Batty, had it painted over after several terrified Fangless drivers accidentally drove into lamp posts.

"Come on, Billy and Bella,

let's sit at the front!" said Lee.

"Uh-oh, here's old Gore. What
does he want?"

Billy and Bella turned to

see Mr E. Gore, the school
caretaker, beetling across
the yard towards them. Mr
Gore was not a vampire
but a zombie. He was also
the gloomiest, grouchiest,
grumpiest and grinchiest
ghoul in town.

"Look," said Lee. "What's
that on Gore's face?"

"It looks like a new nose,"
said Bella. "It's a darker green
than his old one."

"And less warty," said Billy.
"I wonder where he got it
from?"

"Miss Karkoyle! Miss Karkoyle!" hollered Mr Gore. "Shtop! Vait a moment!"

"Oh dear," said Billy nervously. "Do you think he found that stink bomb we left in his boot?"

"Maybe," said Lee. "But he wouldn't dare moan about that. He was fast asleep when he should have been working."

"Miss Karkoyle!" puffed Mr Gore glumly. "Haff you locked the classroom?"

"No, Eric," said Miss Gargoyle coolly. "Why?"

"I must lock it at vonce!" wailed Mr Gore. "All zese robberies in ze town! Another von just last night! Chaney Street First School!

All ze verevolve's face brushes, stolen during a casketball practice!" Chaney Street was the werewolf school down the road. "And zen last veek, at Amenhotep High School, ze spare bandages, all shtolen! Zere vere bits of mummies dropping off everywhere!"

He stroked his new nose,
which was stuck on with a
plaster.

"Aha," said Lee. "So
that's where he got it from."
Amenhotep High School was
the local secondary school for
mummies.

"All zese schools being robbed!"
Mr Gore droned on.

"Alvays at night! Very
suspicious!" He lowered his
voice to a creepy whisper
that was still loud enough for
everyone to hear. "D'you know
sumsink, Miss Karkoyle? I
know who the robbers are!"

"Really?" said Miss
Gargoyle. "Who?"

Mr Gore nodded slyly
towards her class.

"All the robberies are at
night!" he hissed. "And who
comes out at night? Vampires!"

"*And* Fangless burglars," said Miss Gargoyle firmly. "Now we *really* must get going. Goodnight, Eric!"

She climbed onto the bus and sat down.

"Silly old ghoul," said Lee. "Fancy saying vampires might be the robbers."

"I know," said Billy. "If he hates vampires so much, why does he work in a vampire school?"

"Well," said Bella, "he

couldn't get a job in a Fangless school, could he? He'd frighten everyone to death."

"Now, now," said Miss Gargoyle. "Mr Gore's a harmless old soul really. Or he would be, if he had a soul. Anyway, tonight we're going to enjoy ourselves."

Max, the bus driver, started the engine.

"Ready, Miss Gargoyle?"
said Max, fiddling with the
bolt through his neck.

"You bet," she grinned.
"Next stop, the funfair!"

Chapter 2
Pegleg's Castle

The fairground was next to a ruined castle. As the school bus pulled up, the vampires saw large crowds of Fangless folk and all kinds of brightly lit stalls and rides. There were merry-go-rounds, a roller coaster and a big wheel

that was almost as tall as the castle.

"Right," said Miss Gargoyle, as the vampires filed excitedly off the bus. "While we're here I want you all to find out five things about the castle." She held up a pile of papers. "You can write them on these worksheets."

The vampires groaned.

"You mean we actually have to do some *work*?" said Lee.

"That's right," said Miss Gargoyle. "Remember this is a *school* trip. It's meant to be *educational*. You might live in a ruined castle yourselves one day, so it's important to know a bit about them. And the three best worksheets will each win a special prize."

"It's cool, guys," sniggered Big Herb, the laziest boy in the class. "We'll just ask the castle ghosts!"

"No you won't," said Miss Gargoyle. "First, that would be cheating. Second, there *aren't* any ghosts."

"What, a ruined castle with no ghosts?" said Big Herb in disbelief.

"Yes," said Miss Gargoyle. "The castle's last owner was Pegleg Pete, the famous pirate.

He had fifty pet parrots
that made such a
terrible racket no
one could hear the
ghosts wailing and
screeching. So they all moved
out and never came back." She
handed out the worksheets.
"See, I've told you one thing
about the castle already. OK,
now off you go and enjoy
yourselves," she
smiled. "Make
sure you're

back at the bus at midnight. Don't get lost, and don't go flashing your fangs in front of Fangless people. Or turning into bats. The school will get complaints!"

The young vampires all ran gleefully off into the fair.

"Wow!" said Lee "What shall we ride on first?"

"How about the big wheel?" said Bella.

"I don't know," said Billy.
"I'm not very keen on heights."

"Oh, come on," said Lee.
"I'll pay for this one."

They joined the queue for
the big wheel.

"Three rides please," said
Lee, handing over some coins

to a man with shifty eyes and
a thin moustache. The man
took Lee's money and quickly
pushed the children into car
number eight.

"Hey," said Lee. "You didn't
give me any change!"

"Nonsense," sneered the man, locking them in. "Pesky kids. Have a nice ride!" He laughed nastily and before Lee could say anything else, the big wheel whisked them up into the air.

"What a cheat!" fumed Lee, glaring down at the man. "I want my money!"

"Yeah," agreed Bella. "He was *horrid*."

Just then Billy grabbed Bella's arm. They were high above the crowds now and Billy was terrified.

"Oh dear," he quavered, shutting his eyes tight. "I can't bear to look!"

"Why don't you turn into a bat?" said Bella kindly. "You're not scared of heights when you're a bat."

"But Miss Gargoyle said we mustn't!" gabbled Billy.

Suddenly Lee sat up.

"Only in front of Fangless people," he said brightly. "But when we get to the top, no one will see us."

"*Us?*" said Bella. "What do you mean, *us?*"

"I've just had an idea," grinned Lee. "Listen..."

Chapter 3
Bat Trick

Ten minutes later, car number seven came to a halt at the bottom of the big wheel. The man with the thin moustache unlocked the door and a Fangless boy and girl got out. The wheel moved on and car number eight swung down.

"Hur-hur," sneered the man. "Here come those three funny-looking kids I cheated." He unlocked the car. It was empty.

"Eh? Hang on a minute," he gasped. "Where'd they go?"

He looked in, under and on top of the car. Nothing.
He was baffled.
Those kids had
definitely got into
car number eight,
he was sure of it.

Or had they?

Maybe he'd got the number wrong. He waited while all the other cars came down and checked inside every one. But there was no sign of the children. He scratched his moustache, puzzled.

Finally car
number
eight
came
back down
again. The
man couldn't understand it.
Those children had gone up,
so they *must* have come down.
But where were they? All he
could see were three little bats
fluttering high above his head.

There was a long line of
people waiting to get on the

wheel. The man thought hard.

"I'll just take one last look in car number eight," he muttered. "Maybe them pesky kids is hiding under the seat." He crawled into the car on his hands and knees for a closer look. And then three things happened very quickly.

First, the three little bats turned – *POP! POP! POP!* – into three giggling vampires.

Next, one of the vampires – it was Lee – quickly locked

the door of the car with a

SLAM!

Then, Bella
pressed the
green button
that said
START.

"Hey!" yelled the man.
"What's going on? Let me
out!"

But the three vampires just
smiled and waved.

"Have a nice trip," called
Lee, as car number eight

swung into the air. The man
was shouting some *very* rude
words but they grew fainter
and fainter as he rose higher
and higher.

When car number eight
reached the top of the wheel,
Bella pressed the red STOP
button.

"Right," said Lee. "That'll serve him right for cheating people. We'll let him out in half an hour!"

As they left the big wheel, Lee hung a sign on the entrance. It said CLOSED FOR REPAIRS.

"Sorry," said Lee to the waiting Fangless people. "Come back later!"

CLOSED FOR REPAIRS

Chapter 4
Mirror Malarkey

The three vampires wandered around the fair. They bought candyfloss and ice creams, rode on the helter skelter and guessed the weight of a large pig. They also bumped into Lee's werewolf friend Ollie Talbot and his big brother Claude. Ollie and Claude went to Chaney Street First School.

"How come you're off school tonight?" asked Lee.

"It's a blue moon," said Ollie.
"We get a night's holiday."

Ollie and Claude were both
in human form tonight so as
not to terrify Fangless people.
Apart from their hairy hands
they looked just like normal
children.

"We're off for a raw burger," said Ollie. "Coming?"

"No thanks," said Lee. "We just had ice creams. We're on our way to the hall of mirrors."

"OK," said Ollie. "Been on the ghost train yet?"

"No," said Lee. "Maybe we'll

see you there. Fangless ghost trains are always good for a laugh. They're so unscary!"

Lee, Bella and Billy had great fun in the hall of mirrors – until Bella stood next to a Fangless boy who was laughing at his weird reflection in a wobbly mirror.

"Tee-hee!" she chuckled. "You look like a zombie!"

The boy stared at Bella, then at the mirror, then at Bella again. He stopped laughing and his mouth fell open.

"What's wrong?" she asked.
Then she realised. She had
forgotten to turn her reflection
on!

"Oh," she said. "Silly me!
Hang on."

With a *ZZZIP!* Bella's
very wide, wobbly reflection

suddenly appeared in the mirror. The boy gawped even more.

"H-h-how d-d-d-id you d-d-d-d-o that?" he jabbered.

"Oh, it's easy," said Bella. "We learn it at vampire school." She smiled sweetly, showing him her long fangs.

"AAAAAARGGGGH!" screamed the boy. "Mum! Dad! HEEEEEELP!" And he shot out of the hall of mirrors faster than you can say Transylvania.

"What's up with him?" asked Lee.

"I'm not sure," said Bella. "I think it was something I said. Maybe we'd better go."

"Yes," said Billy, looking at his watch. "We've only got another hour and we haven't

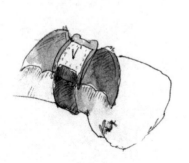

been on the ghost train yet."

"Yikes!" said Lee. "*And* we've got Miss Gargoyle's worksheet to fill in."

"Yes," said Bella. "We'd better do that first."

The three vampires walked to the ruined castle. But when they got there they found the gates chained shut and a big sign that said:

NO ENTRY!
CASTLE HAUNTED!
NASTY GHOSTS AND
GHOULS INSIDE!
KEEP OUT!

Chapter 5
Castle Capers

"That's odd," said Lee. "Miss Gargoyle said there weren't any ghosts."

"Maybe they came back after all," said Bella.

"But why now?" said Billy. "Pegleg Pete's been dead over three hundred years. The ghosts could have returned long ago."

"Mm," said Lee. "It's very strange. Maybe we should take a look."

"But the gates are locked!" said Billy.

"Silly Billy," said Lee. "We'll go in as bats, of course. No one'll notice. Besides, how

else can we do Miss Gargoyle's
worksheet? Come on!"

After checking to make
sure no Fangless people were
watching, they said the bat
chant Miss Gargoyle had
taught them:

"I'm a bat, a bat is me,
A bat is all I want to be."

And with a *POP! POP! POP!*
they all turned into bats and
fluttered off over the castle
wall.

They flew through all the
roofless halls and ruined
chambers of the castle. It was
dark and dank and cold – and
incredibly spooky.

"Wow!" said Lee. "This place is really cool!"

"Yeah," agreed Bella. "I'll bet those old ghosts were sorry to leave!"

"No sign of any *new* ghosts, though," said Lee. "Hang on, what's that?"

They were over some stone steps leading down to the dungeons. At the bottom of the steps was a light!

"Oh dear," quavered Billy. "It's a luminous phantom! I

think we should leave. It's rude to enter another ghoul's home without asking."

"It's not a phantom," said Lee, peering at the light. "It's a fire. Let's take a closer look."

Lee was right. A small campfire was flickering in the dungeon. Next to it were two men.

"It's OK, they're Fangless,"
said Lee.

Hanging from the dungeon
wall was a rusty iron chain.
The vampire bats landed on
it, dangled upside down and
listened.

"Where's Tony? He should
be here by now," growled one
of the men. He was wearing
dark glasses, even though it
was night.

"Dunno, Jim," grunted the other man, who was as big as a truck. "The big wheel stopped ages ago."

Lee grinned at Bella and Billy.

"Tony must be the guy who cheated me!" he whispered.

"Oh dear," said Bella. "I'd forgotten all about him. He's still stuck at the top of the big wheel!"

"But what are they doing in the castle?" wondered Billy.

He didn't have to wait long to find out.

"D'you know what, Milton?" said Jim. "If Tony don't get here soon, we'll just have to rob St. Orlok's without him."

"Yeah," said Jim. "We'll give him ten more minutes, then we go."

The vampire bats nearly fell
off their chain. So that was
it! The three men were the
robbers who'd been burgling
the local schools.
And the castle was their
hideout!

"So that's why we haven't
met a single ghost," said Lee.
"There aren't any!"

"Yes," agreed Bella. "That sign on the castle gate is just a trick to keep everyone away."

"We should tell the Fangless police," said Lee.

"But the men will be gone by the time they get here!" said Billy.

"You're right," said Bella. "It's tricky. We'll have to make sure they don't get away. But how?"

They dangled in silence for a minute. Then Lee spoke.

"I've got an idea," he said, flitting into the air. "I'll explain when I get back. You stay here and keep an eye on the men."

"But where are you going?" cried Bella.

"First I'm going to see Miss Gargoyle," said Lee. "Then I need to find Ollie and Claude…"

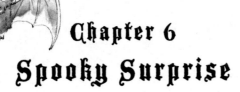

Chapter 6
Spooky Surprise

Lee quickly flew off while Billy and Bella hung in the darkness, keeping an eye on the men.

After about ten minutes Billy said, "Brrr! I wish Lee would hurry up. I'm getting cold. And bored!"

Just then the man called Milton took off his shades and looked at his watch.

"Shh!" whispered Bella.

"He's saying something. Listen!"

"OK. Tony's not here," said the man. "So we're going to have to do it without him." "Right," agreed the man called Jim.

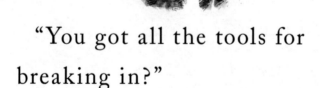

"You got all the tools for breaking in?"

"In the truck with the loot," said the first man. "It's parked at the back of the castle."

"Good," said the other man. "Let's go."

Billy and Bella looked at one another in alarm

"Oh no!" said Billy. "We've got to stop them leaving! But how?"

"There's only one thing for it," said Bella.

"You don't mean...?" gasped Billy.

"Yes," said Bella. "The full vampire works."

"What, fangs and all?" said Billy.

"Yup. Fangs and all."

"But – but Miss Gargoyle said we mustn't!" gasped Billy. "It's against school rules!"

"Look," said Bella. "This is an emergency, right? Miss Gargoyle will understand. It's the only way!"

The two men stood up to go.

"Quick!" said Bella. "You go

and flap in their faces.
That should slow them down a
bit. Hurry!"

Billy didn't need to be asked
twice. The men had almost
reached the dungeon steps.
The man called Milton was in
front and Billy flew straight
at his head, giving his hair a
good ruffling.

"Urgh!" cried the man,
stopping dead so suddenly that

the other man barged right into him. They both tumbled to the ground in a heap.

"Oof!" grunted the second man, picking himself up. "You blinking banana, Milt! Whassamatter?"

"N-nothing," said the first man. "A bat, I think."

The man called Jim sniggered.

"Scared of a tiny bat? You'll be seeing *vampires* next, hur-hur!"

"Too right!" whispered Bella, fluttering over to join Billy in the shadows. "I'll go first."

A few seconds later there was a *POP!*

The noise made both men jump. They squinted in the dark.

"Jim?" whispered the first man. "Look – over there, in the corner! Whassat?"

"I – I dunno, Milt," shivered the other man.

Bella's dark shape was moving silently towards them. She was quite short, but the shadows from the fire made her look much bigger.

POP!

Another shape appeared in the firelight.

"Hey!" called the man named Milton. "What's going on? Who are you?"

"They *look* human," muttered

the other man. "B-but what're
they wearing? Looks like some
sort of cape..."

Staring their scariest stares,
Billy and Bella got closer
and closer and stopped.
Then they slowly raised their
arms, opened their capes and
grinned a pair of huge fangy
grins.

"Arrrrrggghhhh! Vampires! Run!"

The men bolted up the dungeon steps. They hurtled across a courtyard, through a ruined hall and out to the back of the castle, where their truck was waiting. Billy and Bella arrived just in time to see them suddenly screech to a halt. In front of the truck sat a very large dog.

"Blimey," said Milton. "Whose pooch is this? Here boy! Good boy!"

SNARRRRRLLLLL!

Milton hastily backed away.

"OK, OK!" he said nervously.
"N-nice doggy!"

The dog stood on its
hind legs and stared
at them with
big yellow eyes.

It snarled again,
then lifted its
snout and went

HOOOOOOOWWLLLL!

"D-doggy?" jabbered Jim.

"That ain't no dog, Milt.

That's a...

WEREWOLF!

AAAARRRGGHHH!"

The two men ran for their

lives, with the werewolf in hot

pursuit. Billy and Bella were about to follow when a bat flew down to join them. It was Lee. He turned back into a vampire with a *POP!*

"Nice work, you two!" he said. "Ollie's going to chase them to the front gate. Come on!"

The two men didn't stop running till they reached the

gate with the sign on it about ghosts and ghouls.

"Darn it, I forgot we locked it!" cried Jim. "Quick, Milt, gimme the key before those monsters get here!"

"*You've* got the key," quailed Milton. "I gave it to *you*!"

"No, Milt, I gave it to *you*, you numbskull!"

"Did not!"

"Did!"

SNAAAARRRRLLLL!
HOOOOOOOOWLLL!

The men spun around. The werewolf! And now THREE vampires!

Then, out of the shadows by the gatepost, something else appeared. It had its arms out in front and it was wrapped in bandages. And it was stomping towards them, moaning...

"Yowee! A mummy! ARRRGHHH!"

The two robbers kicked and
bashed at the gate until it
finally burst open and they ran
out – straight into the arms of
the police.

A police inspector stepped

forward, with Miss Gargoyle beside him.

"Well, well, well," said the inspector. "If it isn't Milton Grobble and Jim Snark. We've been looking for you for ages. We want to ask you about a few robberies."

"It was us! It was us," wailed Jim. "Just save us from those horrible ghouls!"

"Please put us in prison!" quailed Milton. "The strongest one you got! Anywhere away from those monsters, anywhere!"

"Monsters?" said the inspector. "What monsters?"

"There!" yammered Milton. "Right behind us!"

"Nice try, guys," laughed the inspector. "Hello, kids."

Puzzled, the two robbers slowly turned around. There stood five children – Lee, Bella, Billy, Ollie and Claude.

"Well done, kids," said the inspector. "Your teacher told

us where to wait. Now we just
need to find Tony Kreep, the
third member of the gang."

Lee, Billy and Bella laughed.

"He's at the top of the big
wheel," said Lee. "And all the
loot is in their truck, behind
the castle."

"Excellent," said the
inspector. He looked at
the vampire children and
Miss Gargoyle. "Hey, great
costumes, by the way. Been to
a fancy dress party?"

"Something like that,"
grinned Bella. This time she
was careful *not* to show her
fangs.

The inspector turned to Milton and Jim. "Monsters, huh? Fancy being scared of a bunch of kids!"

All the police officers laughed.

"B-but there *were* monsters!" groaned Milton. "Honest!"

"Tell that to the judge," said the inspector. "Off to prison with them, sergeant."

"The robbers wanted everyone else to think the castle was haunted," said Lee as they got back on the bus. "So I thought *they* might as well think so too!"

"It was great of Ollie and Claude to help out," said Bella. "Claude was a fantastic mummy! Where did he get those bandages?"

"I borrowed them from the first aid tent," said Lee.

"Brilliant!" said Billy.

"Thanks," said Lee. "You
and Bella were brilliant too."

"Well," said Miss Gargoyle.
"You three certainly discovered
a few interesting things about
that castle! I think you deserve

the prizes. Don't you agree, class?"

The whole bus cheered as Miss Gargoyle handed an envelope each to Lee, Bella and Billy. They opened them and gasped in delight.

"Wow!" said Lee. "A ticket to the circus!"

"Doctor Acula's Vampire Spectacula!" cried Bella. "I really wanted to see his show!"

"Me too," said Billy. "But it's

been sold out for months!"

They all chorused "Thanks, Miss Gargoyle!" as Max started the bus and headed back to St. Orlok's.

The End

Hungry for more?

Here's another Vampire School adventure for you to sink your teeth into...

Vampire School
Casketball Capers

Lee, Billy and Bella are all on the St. Orlok's casketball team. (That's the vampire version of basketball, in case you've never played it.) They're all getting ready for a big game against the Chaney Street werewolves. But when the other team arrives, it seems that some of them aren't planning on playing a fair game. Lee needs to come up with a plan – fast! Will he manage to foil the cheats before the final whistle?